HIGH SCHOOL MUSICAL

STORIES FROM EAST HIGH #7

FRIENDS 4 EVER?

By Catherine Hapka

Based on the Disney Channel Original Movie
"High School Musical," Written by Peter Barsocchini

New York

visit us at www.abdopublishing.com

Reinforced library bound edition published in 2010 by Spotlight, a division of ABDO Group, 8000 West 78th Street, Edina, Minnesota 55439. This edition reprinted by arrangement with Disney Press, an imprint of Disney Book Group, LLC. www.disneybooks.com

Library of Congress Cataloging-in-Publication Data

Grace, N. B.
High school musical stories from East High / by N. B. Grace ; based on the Disney channel original movie "High School Musical," written by Peter Barsocchini. -- Reinforced library bound ed.
 v. cm.
 Contents: [1] Broadway dreams -- [2] Friends 4ever? -- [3] Get your vote on! -- [4] Heart to heart -- [5] Ringin' it in -- [6] Turn up the heat.
 ISBN 978-1-59961-633-9 (v. 1) -- ISBN 978-1-59961-634-6 (v. 2) -- ISBN 978-1-59961-635-3 (v. 3) -- ISBN 978-1-59961-636-0 (v. 4) -- ISBN 978-1-59961-637-7 (v. 5) -- ISBN 978-1-59961-638-4 (v. 6)
 I. Barsocchini, Peter, 1952- II. High school musical (Motion picture) III. Title.
PZ7.G75149Hi 2010
[E]--dc22

                              2009002935

All Spotlight books have reinforced library binding and are manufactured in the United States of America.

CHAPTER ONE

"Gabriella Montez!" Principal Matsui called out. "Just the student I wanted to see!"

Gabriella looked up from her locker as she shuffled through the papers in her chemistry notebook. She had a quiz that day, and she wanted to make sure she had her notes so she could do a little extra cramming during homeroom.

The principal of East High was smiling at her from behind his wire-rimmed glasses. Beside him was a tall girl with strawberry blonde hair and freckles. Gabriella had never seen her before.

"Hi, Principal Matsui," Gabriella said, closing her locker. "What's up?"

"Gabriella Montez, this is Ashley Appleton," the principal said, motioning to the girl beside him. "She just moved here from Michigan."

"Oh! Hi, Ashley. Welcome to East High." Gabriella smiled warmly at the girl. She had been the new girl plenty of times in her life, and she knew exactly how unnerving it could be to face a whole school full of strangers.

"Thanks," Ashley said. "It seems pretty cool here so far."

"Yes, yes." Principal Matsui rubbed his hands together. "I'm sure you'll find East High very, er, cool, Ashley. Gabriella is in your homeroom, so I thought perhaps she wouldn't mind showing you around today." He smiled at Gabriella. "Miss Montez was the new girl in school herself not too long ago, so I know she'll treat you right."

"Sure," Gabriella said. "I'd be happy to show you around, Ashley. Did anyone show you how to get to homeroom yet?"

"Not yet." Ashley giggled. "I just hope I don't get totally lost. East High is a lot bigger than my old school."

Principal Matsui checked his watch. "Better hurry, girls," he said. "The bell rings in fifteen minutes."

He hurried off toward his office. Gabriella turned and led the way down the hall in the opposite direction. "It's too bad you had to switch schools in the middle of the semester," she said sympathetically. "That's really hard."

"Tell me about it!" Ashley rolled her eyes. "My dad's company was so totally spastic about getting us here that I couldn't even convince him to let me stay in Michigan an extra two weeks for my friend Samantha's birthday ski trip. It's probably going to be the party of the century, and I have to miss it!"

Gabriella had never been all that interested in

parties—or skiing, for that matter. But she understood how Ashley must be feeling.

"I know what you mean," she said. "When my mom got transferred from Illinois to San Diego, we had to move right before I was supposed to go on this cool field trip to the science museum in Chicago. Oh! And the move before that?" She grimaced at the memory. "That one happened two weeks before my birthday."

Ashley shot her a curious look. "Whoa, it sounds like you've moved almost as much as me."

"Eight schools in eleven and a half years." Gabriella smiled ruefully.

"Only five schools here." Ashley laughed and held up both hands. "You win!"

Gabriella giggled. "Trust me, that's one award I'd love to give back! Still, it wasn't so bad. At least I ended up at East High. You're going to love it here—it's a really great school." She checked her watch. "We'd better hurry. The bell's going to ring soon."

* * *

"Another Monday morning." Chad Danforth groaned, spinning the basketball he was holding on one finger as he walked down the packed school hallway. "That means another whole week of school before our next game."

Troy Bolton grinned at his friend. As far as Chad was concerned, every Monday morning was cause for, well, mourning.

"Look on the bright side," Troy said. "That gives us five nights of practice before we face Jefferson High this weekend."

"Yeah. We gotta keep our streak going." Chad raised one hand for a high five. "Go Wildcats!"

Troy returned the high five. The East High Wildcats had won their last nine games in a row. It was the team's longest winning streak in several years.

"And Jefferson High is tough," Troy said. "We're going to have to really be on top of our game—"

"Troy! Yoo-hoo, Troy!"

Troy glanced over his shoulder. Sharpay Evans was rushing down the hall toward him, pushing her way through the throng of students. He winced as she accidentally whacked someone with her rhinestone-studded designer purse. Her matching shoes click-clacked loudly on the tile floor. Sharpay was co-president of the East High drama club, and just about everything she did was . . . *dramatic.*

"Hi, Sharpay," he said as she skidded to a stop in front of him. "How was your weekend?"

"Never mind that." Sharpay waved one manicured hand in the air as if the question were no more important than a pesky mosquito. "Troy, I wanted you to be among the first to hear my big announcement."

Chad was staring at Sharpay's candy-pink-striped outfit and glitter eye shadow. "What—that the clown look is making a comeback?"

Sharpay made a sour face at Chad. But she broke into a smile again as she returned her attention to Troy. "I'm sure you both realize my birthday is this weekend," she said. "Oh, and Ryan's, too, of course."

"How did I miss the news bulletin?" Chad wondered out loud.

As usual, Sharpay grandly ignored Chad's gibe. "To celebrate, I'll be hosting a sophisticated little soiree at the country club this Saturday night. *Very* exclusive, of course."

"Of course," Troy said.

Chad tossed his basketball from one hand to the other. "So don't keep us in suspense, Sharpay," he said. "Who made the cut?"

"All in due time, my little basketball-bouncing friend. All in due time." Sharpay winked at Troy. "After all, what's the fun of an exclusive guest list if I blurt it out just like that?" She waggled one finger and shook her head. "Sorry, boys. That wouldn't do at all. There will be a formal announcement later this week."

"Well, I'm sure the party will be fun, Sharpay," Troy said politely.

"Oh, trust me, Troy. It will be an evening to remember." Sharpay patted her blonde hair and shot both guys a self-satisfied smile. "That's why I wanted to give you the opportunity to save the date. See, a little bird told me that you just *might* make the cut." Her smile faded slightly as she glanced at Chad. "You, too, Troy's friend. Maybe."

"Cool. But my boy and I will have to play it by ear." Chad slung one arm over Troy's shoulder. "See, when party time rolls around, we might still be busy celebrating our winning streak hitting double digits." He backed away and spun his basketball at Troy.

Troy caught it and laughed. "No problem," he said. "We can just make it a combo birthday party and victory celebration."

Sharpay didn't look entirely pleased by that idea, but she smiled and gave them a little wave. "I'll keep you boys posted," she said over her shoulder as she hurried off.

"You do that," Chad said.

Troy dribbled the ball on the hall floor, then shot it back at Chad. Chad was a little too slow, and it bounced off his fingertips and crashed into a locker door.

"Yo, man, you'll have to do better than that if we want to keep our winning streak alive!" Troy called, still laughing as Chad scrambled after the ball.

But he was only joking. The Wildcats had Friday's game in the bag!

CHAPTER TWO

"**R**eady for the last stop on your whirlwind tour of East High?" Gabriella asked as she and Ashley hurried down the crowded hallway.

"Sure," Ashley said. "But I'm not expecting much. Nothing could be more exciting than the book-return slot outside the library."

Gabriella laughed. It was easy to see that Ashley was a lot more interested in the outdoor patio, the mirrors in the girls' restroom, and even the wildcat statue in the upstairs lobby than she was in the library, the chemistry lab, or anything else having to do with actual academic activities. Obviously, she and Gabriella had different ideas about what was important in a school.

"You're right, it probably won't be that exciting," Gabriella said. "But anyway, here it is—your new homeroom."

She led the way inside. Most of the class was already there. Gabriella's friend Taylor McKessie was bent over a textbook at her desk. Troy was lounging against the wall talking to his friends Zeke Baylor and Jason Cross, who were sitting with their long legs sprawling out into the aisle. Chad was nearby, practicing some moves with the basketball he carried around everywhere.

"Whoa!" Ashley's eyes widened, and she pursed her pink-glossed lips. "Who's the mega-hottie?"

Following her gaze, Gabriella realized Ashley was staring at Troy and his friends. "Um, you mean the dark-haired kid in the back row?" she said. "His name's Jason, and he—"

"No." Ashley cut her off. "I mean Mr. Gorgeous there in the blue T-shirt. I thought we had some cute guys at my last school, but now I'm wishing I moved here ages ago!"

Gabriella could feel heat rising in her cheeks as she realized Ashley was talking about Troy.

This is awkward with a capital A! she thought. Still, she realized the new girl had no way of knowing that Troy and Gabriella were an item.

"Um, that's Troy," she said. "He and I—well, that is, Troy is, um . . ."

Ashley continued staring at Troy for a moment as Gabriella stammered. Then she finally glanced over. Her eyes widened, and her mouth rounded into a little O.

"Omigosh!" she hissed in a stage whisper. "You mean you and Troy . . ."

Gabriella shrugged and nodded, positive that her cheeks were bright red by now. "Sorry."

"No, I'm the one who's sorry!" Ashley grabbed her arm and squeezed it. "I swear, Gabriella, I never would've said anything if I knew he was your guy. Let's just hit rewind and pretend it never happened, okay?"

Gabriella's shoulders slumped in relief. The awkward moment had passed, just like that.

"Deal," she said with a smile. "Now, where were we? Oh, yeah—welcome to your new homeroom."

"Thanks," Ashley said, returning her smile. "It's nice to walk into homeroom with a friend for a change."

A friend? Gabriella's smile widened. She liked the sound of that.

Okay, so maybe Ashley and I don't seem to have a whole lot in common other than the moving thing, she thought. So what? A lot of people wouldn't have thought Troy and I had much in common at first, and look at us now.

Just then, Taylor looked up and spotted Gabriella. She waved and hurried over.

"Hey," she said. "Did you study for that chem quiz?" She blinked, suddenly seeming to notice

Ashley for the first time. "Oh. Hi there."

Gabriella introduced the two girls. "Taylor is the captain of our Scholastic Decathlon team," Gabriella said.

"Scholastic what?" Ashley said with a giggle. "Is that, like, juggling books or something?" Without waiting for an answer, she pointed toward Chad, who had just sunk a "basket" in the classroom's trash can. "Hey, are those guys on the basketball team? I love basketball! My old school had an awesome team."

"So does your new school," Gabriella told her. "The Wildcats are on a nine-game winning streak right now."

"Cool!" Ashley said, sounding genuinely impressed.

Just then Chad looked over and saw her staring. "Yo," he said, loping over. "Who's your cute new friend, ladies?"

Ashley giggled and tilted her head. "I love your hair," she said, gazing up at Chad. "It's so wild!"

Out of the corner of her eye, Gabriella could

see that Taylor was scowling. She and Chad were an on-again, off-again couple. As far as Gabriella knew, at the moment they were supposed to be on again.

Uh-oh, she thought, wincing. Oh, well, I'm sure Ashley will back off when she figures things out, just like she did with Troy. She's just trying to be friendly and fit in, that's all.

"Come on, Ashley," she said. "Taylor and I will introduce you to the other guys."

"I'll have to take a rain check," Taylor said, still looking annoyed. "I want to do a little more studying for that chemistry quiz."

"That's my girl," Chad joked. "Always exercising that supersize brain."

"Right," Taylor said. "*Some* people could use a little more of that kind of exercise." She spun on her heel and headed for her desk.

"Hey, what'd I do this time?" Chad exclaimed, hurrying after her.

"Oops." Ashley stared after them. "Was it something I said?"

"Don't worry about them. They're always like that." Gabriella led the way over to Troy and the others. "Hi, you guys," she said, interrupting their spirited discussion of last weekend's basketball game.

Troy looked up. "Hey!" he said, his face brightening as soon as he saw her. That expression always made Gabriella flash back to the first time they'd met—the first time they'd sung together. That had been such a special moment, and things had only gotten better between them since then.

"Hi," she said, smiling at him. "This is Ashley. She's new. Ashley, this is Jason and that's Zeke. And this is Troy."

"Nice to meet you," Ashley said. "I hear you guys are, like, basketball *gods*."

"That's us," Jason said, puffing up his chest playfully. "Masters of the universe."

Zeke smacked his friend on the shoulder and laughed. "Get real, man. You didn't look like a master of anything when you tripped over your shoelace and wiped out last weekend in front of the whole crowd."

"Oh, yeah? I did that on purpose to make everyone forget that rebound you fumbled, dude," Jason retorted with a grin.

"Boys, boys, no need to argue," Troy put in. "You're *both* master dorks."

As the guys continued to joke around, making Ashley laugh, Gabriella sneaked a peek at her watch. It was almost time for the warning bell.

Oh, well, she thought. Guess I won't have time to do any extra cramming, after all. . . .

"Excuse me, people!" a loud voice announced. "May I have your attention, please?"

Gabriella looked up and saw Sharpay posed dramatically in the doorway. Her brother, Ryan, was right behind her. Everyone else in the classroom stopped talking and glanced over.

"Thank you!" Sharpay took a few steps into the room. She put one hand on her chest. "I'm very sorry, but I'm going to have to insist that everyone quit begging me to tell them whether they're invited to my very exclusive party this Saturday night. I'm afraid you'll all have to wait to find out. It just wouldn't be fair to tell some people and not others."

"Right," Ryan spoke up. "Not fair at all."

Sharpay shot her brother a slightly annoyed look. "Yes," she said. "As I was saying, I must insist upon my privacy. That is all." She flounced to her seat, sat down, and pulled out her cell phone.

"What was all that about?" Gabriella asked as the rest of the class starting buzzing about Sharpay's announcement. "What party?"

Troy shook his head and smiled. "Some birthday party she's having at the country club," he said. "I guess it's supposed to be some big, fancy, exclusive event for everyone who's anyone at East High. Or something like that." He winked at Gabriella.

Gabriella grinned. That sounded just like Sharpay. She loved being center stage, whether there was a play going on at the time or not.

"Really?" Ashley glanced over at Sharpay with interest. "That sounds cool. And I really love her outfit—maybe I should go tell her that. Want to introduce me, Gabriella?"

"Trust me," Jason told her with a smirk. "You don't want to meet Sharpay any sooner than you have to."

Ashley ignored him. "Please?" she wheedled, smiling hopefully at Gabriella. "I just feel like I should get to know as many people as I can, you know? And you've been so great about introducing me around. . . ."

Gabriella hesitated. She and Sharpay had never exactly been the best of friends. Gabriella had barely been at East High a week when she'd won the lead in the school musical—a part Sharpay had been certain belonged to her. It also didn't help that Sharpay had always had a crush on Troy, and that he hadn't had eyes for anyone else since Gabriella arrived on the scene.

Still, the two of them had reached some sort of

understanding since then. And what was the harm in introducing Ashley? She'd figure out for herself soon enough that a little Sharpay went a long way.

"Well, okay, I guess," Gabriella said.

"Thanks, Gabriella!" Ashley smiled. She waggled her fingers at Troy and his friends. "Catch you guys later, okay? I want to hear all about this weekend's game."

She and Gabriella headed for Sharpay's desk. Sharpay had put away her cell phone and was talking to Ryan.

"Excuse me, Sharpay?" Gabriella said when they reached her.

Sharpay sighed loudly. "Did you not hear what I just said?" she exclaimed. "If you're here about the party . . ."

"I'm not," Gabriella assured her quickly. "I just wanted you to meet Ashley. She's new."

"I see." Sharpay looked Ashley up and down with obvious disdain.

"Hi, Sharpay," Ashley said eagerly. "I'm

really sorry for interrupting. I just wanted Gabriella to introduce me so I could tell you that your jacket is absolutely awesome!"

"Oh." Sharpay seemed surprised. But she smiled and smoothed down the lapels of her pink striped top. "Thanks."

"It's a designer original, actually," Ryan put in.

"It looks great on you, Sharpay," Ashley gushed. "I also really, really love your hair. How do you get it so smooth and shiny?"

Sharpay tossed her head, making her blonde locks bounce. "Well, actually, I—" she began.

"Excuse me, but I'd better go—I just remembered I need to study for a quiz," Gabriella interrupted. Without waiting for a response, she scooted off across the room. The last thing she felt like doing was hanging around to listen to Sharpay expound upon her favorite subject— herself.

If Ashley's already a Sharpay fan, Gabriella thought ruefully, maybe that means we have even less in common than I thought.

"Hey, good move," Troy said, grabbing her by the hand as she walked by and pulling her down into the seat behind him. Then he leaned toward her with a playful smile. "You finally ditched the newbie."

Gabriella smiled back uncertainly, feeling a twinge of guilt at his words. Ditched the newbie? Was that what she'd just done?

"What's that supposed to mean?" she teased back. "I was the newbie once myself, don't you remember?"

"Yeah. But you were different." He grinned. "Much cuter, for one thing."

Gabriella blushed at the sweet words. "Nice." She pretended to be dismayed, even though she knew Troy was only joking. "It's a good thing poor Ashley has me, or her new life at East High would be sad and lonely."

She was mostly kidding—Ashley didn't seem like the type of person to be lonely for long. But Gabriella wasn't going to take any chances. Troy, Taylor, and her other friends at East High had made her early days here much less confusing and lonely than they had been at any of her other schools. And she was planning to do her best to pay it forward by doing the same for Ashley.

CHAPTER THREE

"**H**ey," Troy greeted Chad, who was cramming his schoolbooks into his already overstuffed locker. "How'd you do on that chem quiz today?"

Chad groaned. "Don't ask!"

He slammed the locker shut. It took two or three tries, but finally the latch clicked. Then he tucked his basketball under his arm and slung his gym bag over the other shoulder.

Troy grinned. "Dude, one of these days your locker is going to explode. And it's not going to be pretty."

"Funny. You sound just like Taylor." Chad grimaced. "She actually wrote out some equation proving that if I jammed one more thing in there, the total mass would be too much for the volume of pi squared times x. Or some sciencey junk like that." He rolled his eyes. "Can you believe her?"

"What I can't believe is that you two can put up with each other," Troy countered, his grin widening. He and Gabriella might have started out as a little bit of an odd couple—nobody would have predicted that the captain of the basketball team would fall for a math-and-science genius. But Chad and Taylor were an even weirder match.

Troy and Chad headed down the hall. Last period had just ended, and students were at their lockers or rushing off to after-school activities or to catch the bus. Troy checked his watch to see how much time they had before basketball practice started. The coach—who also happened to be Troy's dad—hated it when his players were late.

As they rounded a corner, Troy spotted Gabriella at her locker. That new girl, Ashley, was with her. Ashley spotted the two guys right away.

"Hi, Troy! Hi, Chad! Off to practice?" she called as they approached.

"You got it," Chad replied. "We've got to get ready to dominate Jefferson High this Saturday." He tossed his basketball in the air and spun around, catching it in his other hand.

Gabriella just smiled, but Ashley clapped enthusiastically. "That was great!" she exclaimed. "I'm starting to understand why you guys are so good."

"Uh-huh," Troy said. He glanced at his watch again. "And one way we stay that way is by showing up for practice on time. Come on, Chad, let's get going."

"Bye," Gabriella said.

"See you." Troy smiled at her, then hurried off.

Chad caught up around the next corner. "Yo,

what's the rush?" he said. "We don't have to be on the court for fifteen minutes." He grabbed Troy by the arm and his eyes widened. "Hold on a sec," he said. "This . . . this doesn't mean . . ."

"What?" Troy hid a smile. He could tell Chad was goofing off again.

Chad put a hand to his forehead, pretending he was about to faint. The basketball slipped out of his other hand and rolled down the hall.

"It's finally happened!" he exclaimed, dramatically enough to do Sharpay proud. "You're finally over Gabriella!"

Troy shook his head and grinned. "Sorry, wrong answer." His smile faded, and he glanced back over his shoulder to make sure the girls were nowhere in sight. "But now that you mention it, I *am* sort of over that new girl."

"Ashley?" Chad looked surprised. "What's your problem with her? She seems pretty cool."

"You like anyone who thinks you're a basketball god," Troy joked. He scooped up Chad's basketball and tossed it from hand to hand.

"And you're right. Ashley is perfectly nice. It's just that she's been sticking to Gabriella like glue all day and acting like her new best friend or something. . . ." He hesitated, not really sure what he was trying to say. Usually Troy got along with just about everybody, but there was something about the new girl that rubbed him the wrong way.

Chad shrugged. "Okay, so maybe Ashley's trying a little too hard," he said. "But give her a chance, bro. Sometimes people grow on you. Kind of like a fungus."

Troy smiled. "Thinking about Taylor again, huh?" he joked.

"Funny," Chad said. "Seriously, though. Give it some time. At least it's not like Gabriella's spending all this time with another guy, right?"

Troy blinked. "It's not that," he said, realizing that Chad thought he was jealous of all the time Gabriella was spending with the new girl. That wasn't it—was it?

He bit his lip. Suddenly he wasn't sure. Maybe

I am just jealous, he thought. And that's not fair to Ashley—or Gabriella, either. Why shouldn't she make a new friend if she wants to? I probably just need to try a little harder to see whatever it is she sees in Ashley, that's all.

He tossed the basketball back to Chad. "Come on. We'd better keep moving or we really are going to be late for practice."

"Someday, maybe, I'll figure out my way around this place!" Ashley cried. "I still can't believe I walked into the teachers' lounge during free period, thinking it was the language lab!"

Gabriella smiled. "Give yourself a break," she said. "It's only been one day. You'll figure it out."

The two girls had just finished at their lockers. Now Gabriella was walking Ashley out before heading to her Scholastic Decathlon meeting, which was scheduled to start half an hour after the final bell.

"Are you sure you have to go to that meeting?" Ashley asked. "We could grab a soda or go shopping or something instead. Wouldn't that be a lot more fun?"

"Sorry. They're expecting me at the meeting," Gabriella said. "You could come with me if you want, though."

Ashley shuddered. "No, thanks," she said. "I'm allergic to brainiacs." She shot Gabriella an apologetic grin. "Present company excluded, of course."

Before Gabriella could answer, she heard a commotion from around the corner. "That sounds like Sharpay," she murmured. "And she doesn't sound happy."

Ashley's eyes brightened. "Do you think it's about that party?" she whispered. "Let's eavesdrop!"

The two of them crept to the corner and peered around. Sharpay and Ryan were standing in an otherwise-empty hall facing each other. Sharpay's eyes were flashing fire, and Ryan had an anxious look on his face.

". . . and when I called the florist, they said you

hadn't even contacted them yet to place the order!" Sharpay was shouting. "I can't believe you dropped the ball on this! You know the right flowers can make or break a party, and it's not easy to get orchids on less than a week's notice!"

"I know, I know," Ryan said. "But I told you, I really needed to study for that chemistry quiz yesterday, and—"

"That's no excuse for ruining my—I mean, *our*—big night!" Sharpay crossed her arms over her chest. "If I didn't know better, I'd think you were more interested in stupid stuff like your homework than you are in making this party a success." She started ticking things off on her fingers. "You forgot about the flowers. You told the caterers buffet-style when you knew I wanted sit-down service. You haven't even finished designing the ice sculpture, or . . ."

"Yikes," Ashley whispered in Gabriella's ear as Sharpay's rant continued. "She's serious about this party, isn't she?"

Gabriella flashed her a smile, but didn't say

anything. She felt a little guilty about spying and didn't want Sharpay to hear them.

"That's not true," Ryan told his sister weakly. "I do care about the party. But I don't want to flunk out of school."

Sharpay ignored that. Her expression turned thoughtful. "You know, I wonder if I need to jazz up the plans a little more," she mused aloud. "Unfortunately, you're not the only one who isn't paying nearly enough attention to this party. I really need to come up with something that will get people talking. Add some pizzazz."

She started pacing, tapping her chin with one finger. Ryan watched her go back and forth, his head moving from side to side like a spectator at a tennis match.

"Like what?" he asked.

Sharpay stopped short, her face lighting up. "I've got it!" she crowed. "We could kick things off with a big, splashy musical number. Kind of a way to welcome everyone to the party, you know?

You could choreograph it, and we could hire a live band to accompany us. . . ."

Gabriella could feel laughter bubbling up inside her. She grabbed Ashley and dragged her back around the corner. They hurried down the hall, managing to make it halfway to the next corner before bursting into giggles.

"A musical number?" Ashley exclaimed. "Is she serious?"

"Unfortunately, yes." Gabriella shook her head. "Sharpay can't imagine anything more exciting than other people getting to watch her sing."

Ashley glanced back over her shoulder. "Still, I bet it's going to be an awesome party," she said, sounding a bit wistful. "It sounds like she's going all out with the flowers and the caterer and everything. . . . I mean, I've never even been to a party with an ice sculpture before! Aren't you dying to know if you'll make the guest list, Gabriella?"

"Not really." Gabriella shrugged. "If she

invites me, I'll go. If she doesn't, I'll do something else. No big deal."

"But this will be the party of the century!" Ashley cried. "How can you not care about whether you're invited?"

"I guess because I know Sharpay," Gabriella joked. She could tell that Ashley really wanted to go to that party, and she wanted to make her feel better if she didn't make the cut. "She talks a good game, but what's that saying in show business? All sizzle and no bacon?" She smiled. "I have a feeling this party might just be a *lot* of sizzle."

"Really?" Ashley didn't look convinced. "Well, I still think it will be—"

"Clear the way!" a shout came from the end of the hall. A second later Chad and Jason raced around the corner, looking panicky.

"What's wrong?" Gabriella called to them as they hurried past.

"It's Troy!" Jason called over his shoulder, not slowing his pace. "He's hurt—bad!"

CHAPTER FOUR

Troy hobbled into the school lobby trying not to catch his crutches on the threshold. He kept his gaze on the floor ahead of him, but even so, he was aware that people were staring from every direction. Chad and Zeke flanked him on either side, and Jason walked a few steps behind, carrying Troy's books.

"Careful, man," Chad said, grabbing Troy's arm as one of the crutches slipped slightly on the smooth floor. "You don't want to wipe out and mess up your other ankle, too."

Troy shook off his friend's hand. "I'm okay."

He still couldn't believe he'd landed funny after that rebound and sprained his ankle. Practice hadn't even officially started yet—it had happened during the warm-up. At first everyone had thought it was broken, but luckily the x-rays had showed it was merely a sprain.

"How long did the doc say it would be until you can play again?" Jason asked.

Troy sighed. "Three weeks," he replied. "Minimum."

"It could be worse," Zeke said. "When my cousin sprained her ankle, they told her she couldn't do ballet again for two months."

"Gee, that's looking on the bright side," Chad told him, rolling his eyes. "Three weeks or ten years, who cares? The Jefferson game is in four days!"

"I know," Troy moaned. "I can't believe I have to sit it out. I'll never forgive myself if we blow our winning streak because of this."

Just then a gaggle of cheerleaders in their perky red uniforms spotted Troy. They rushed over and flocked around him, their faces filled with concern.

"How are you feeling Troy?" one asked.

"I was *so* upset when I heard you got hurt!" another cried.

"You and me both," Troy muttered, feeling frustrated and a little sheepish.

The cheerleaders were still clustered around the boys when Gabriella entered the lobby with Ashley. She quickly spotted Troy in the middle of the group.

"There he is," she told Ashley. "I'm going to go see how he's doing."

Gabriella hadn't seen Troy since he'd been carried out of the gym, but she'd spoken with him on the phone. It was a relief that his injury hadn't turned out to be as severe as everyone had feared. But she was still worried about him. He lived for basketball—knowing that he couldn't play for several weeks had to be tough on him.

And I'm sure it doesn't help that the whole school is already buzzing about Saturday's game, she thought. Everyone seems more worried about how this might affect that winning streak than they are about poor Troy!

"Hi," Gabriella said as she and Ashley reached the group around Troy. The cheerleaders parted to let them through, and Gabriella reached out to touch one of his crutches. "How are you doing? It looks like you're getting around okay."

Troy smiled. "I feel like an idiot," he said. "Who sprains their ankle during warm-ups, anyway?"

"Don't be too hard on yourself," Gabriella told him. "It could happen to anyone."

"I guess," Troy said, though he didn't seem convinced. "Hi, Ashley," he added. "How's it going?"

"Hi, Troy," Ashley said. "Total bummer about your ankle."

"Thanks. So I didn't get a chance to ask while

they were carrying me out on that stretcher—how was your first day at East High?"

Gabriella smiled. That was just like Troy. Even in the midst of his own problems, he was still so thoughtful!

Ashley was still chattering on about her impressions of East High when the whole group reached homeroom. Troy was trying to pretend he was listening to her. He'd seen Gabriella flash him that gorgeous smile when he'd asked after Ashley. He was glad she'd noticed his attempts to be nice to the new girl.

I should have plenty of chances to get to know Ashley over the next few weeks, he thought with a sigh. *After all, I'll have lots of time that I won't be spending playing basketball. . . .*

"Injured man coming through!" Chad sang out as Troy limped across the room. "Make way, people."

Troy collapsed into his seat. The crowd around him was growing by the moment. Gossip traveled fast at East High, and everyone wanted to get a look at the splint on Troy's ankle.

"So how'd it happen?" a girl asked. "I heard you tripped over Chad and crashed into the bleachers."

"I heard you were going for a slam dunk and landed on Zeke," another girl said.

Troy shook his head. "Not quite," he said. "It was just a stupid, bad step on a rebound, that's all." He glanced around at his teammates. "Unfortunately, I'm not the only one who's going to be paying for it. You guys will just have to make up for me not being able to play on Saturday."

"Don't sweat it, man," Zeke said. "We'll work it out."

Troy stared at him thoughtfully. "Yeah," he said. "If Jefferson High senses any weakness, they'll come at us twice as hard. So Zeke, you're going to have to pick up the slack in rebounds. Jason, you'll have to really hustle on defense. And Chad—"

Chad laughed and slapped Troy on the back.

"Good old Troy," he said. "Always worried about the team!"

"Aha! So this is where everybody is."

Troy glanced over. Sharpay had just entered the classroom with Ryan at her heels.

"Troy!" she exclaimed, striding toward his desk. "Glad to see you were able to join us today after your little accident. I trust your knee is feeling better?"

"It's my ankle, actually," Troy said. "And it's feeling a little better already. Thanks for asking." Knowing Sharpay, Troy suspected she was annoyed that everyone was paying more attention to his injury than to her upcoming party. But to his surprise, she didn't look upset at all. In fact, there was an odd twinkle in her eyes and a smug smile playing around the corners of her mouth.

Sharpay turned to face the rest of the class and cleared her throat. "I have an announcement that just might interest everyone enough to drag you all away from Troy's little medical drama," she said. "So listen up!"

"Let me guess," Chad said. "You're finally going to tell us who's invited to your tea party."

Sharpay shot him an irritated look. "Hardly," she said. "In fact, considering what I'm about to tell you, I'm going to have to be even more selective about who makes the cut."

"What is it, Sharpay?" Ashley cried excitedly.

Sharpay's gaze drifted to her. "Um, and you are . . . ?" she said.

"She's Ashley," Gabriella said. "You met her yesterday, remember?"

"Oh, right." Sharpay shrugged. "It must have slipped my mind. See, I've had a lot going on the past couple of days—"

"If you've got big news, just spill it already!" Jason called out.

"Well!" Sharpay tilted her nose in the air, looking insulted. "If you're going to be *that* way about it, maybe you don't want to hear my news after all."

Ryan jumped forward, practically quivering

with excitement. "Oh, but you have to tell them, Sharpay!" he cried. "This is huge news! Trina Chica—"

"Hush!" Sharpay hissed before her brother could say anything else.

Up until that moment, most of the class had been paying only moderate attention to Sharpay. But now she had everyone's full attention.

"Trina Chica?" Jason exclaimed. "What about her?"

"Man, she rocks!" Chad cried. "Have you seen her new video?"

Ashley nodded. "She's totally my favorite singer in the whole world!"

Sharpay spoke up again, her stage-trained voice cutting through the hubbub easily. "Well, then," she said, "you all might be interested to know that Trina Chica herself will be appearing at my party on Saturday night."

CHAPTER FIVE

"**W**hoa!" Troy exclaimed. "Trina Chica is going to be at your party? Really?"

Gabriella was impressed, too. Trina Chica was one of the hottest singers around. Her new album had gone double platinum, and her concert tour had just kicked off in New York City a few weeks earlier. Could she really be performing at Sharpay's party? It seemed too good to be true.

But if anybody can make something like that happen, it's Sharpay, Gabriella thought. She has a way of getting what she wants. And what she wants right now is a party that everyone will remember forever.

The buzz in the classroom was now an uproar. "Yes," Sharpay said, obviously pleased with the reaction. "I thought you all might find that interesting."

By the time Gabriella, Taylor, and Ashley had left homeroom for first period, the entire school had heard the big news. Sharpay was mobbed by excited Trina Chica fans as soon as she stepped into the hall.

"This is going to be quite a week. People are already acting crazy about this Trina Chica thing," Taylor commented as she dodged several squealing underclassmen who were flinging themselves at Sharpay.

"Can you blame them?" Ashley shivered with delight and wrapped her arms around herself. "I mean, Trina Chica! How cool is that?" She sighed loudly. "I just *have* to figure out how to get an invite to that party!"

"I wouldn't get too worked up about it if I were you," Taylor advised. "It's not worth it."

"Are you kidding?" Ashley looked genuinely surprised at Taylor's comment. "Gabriella, back me up here—don't you want to see Trina perform live?"

"Not enough to start stressing over a party invitation," Gabriella replied honestly. "I mean, sure, it would be cool to see Trina Chica. I've heard she puts on a great live show—they're even showing one of her concerts as a TV special sometime soon." She shrugged. "But Sharpay is going to invite whoever she wants to invite. I'm not going to worry about it."

Taylor smirked. "Easy for you to say. You know your name is definitely going to be on that short list, Gabriella."

"Really?" Ashley stared at Gabriella curiously. "I thought you and Sharpay weren't that close."

"They're not," Taylor replied before Gabriella could even say a word. "But Sharpay has been crushing on Troy Bolton since the sixth grade. She may be a little, um, self-involved, but she's not stupid—she knows if she wants Troy to come to her party, she'd better invite Gabriella, too." She shot Gabriella an amused look. "Your name will be on that list, my friend. Take it to the bank."

Gabriella smiled sheepishly. "You're probably right," she said. "I hadn't really thought of it that way."

"Wow," Ashley said, a note of envy in her voice. "Gabriella, I just hope you realize how lucky you are. And I hope you'll think of me while you're grooving to Trina's music on Saturday night—and maybe get me an autograph?"

"Sure," Gabriella said. She couldn't help feeling sorry for Ashley, especially when she remembered what the new girl had told her about missing her friend's party back home. That had to make the whole Sharpay situation even worse for her. "I'll do what I can."

* * *

47

Troy slumped in his chair, staring into space. It was third period, and Ms. Darbus had been droning on and on about some boring old Greek play for the past twenty minutes. But Troy wasn't listening. All he could think about was the coming game against Jefferson High.

How could I have done something so stupid? he thought, his gaze wandering to the crutches leaning against the wall nearby. I really blew it this time. If our winning streak ends this Saturday, it will be all my fault.

He clenched his fists, wishing he could go back in time and land on the other foot or some-thing after grabbing that rebound. Since that wasn't possible, he started trying to figure out how to make things better now. The doctor who had splinted his injured ankle had given him some strengthening exercises to do. He wasn't supposed to start them until a few days had passed, but he figured the sooner the better.

Might as well get a jump on it, right? Troy told himself. Maybe if I work hard enough, I'll be okay in time for our game against West High the week after next.

Having a plan of action made him feel a lot better. Checking to make sure Ms. Darbus wasn't looking his way, he stretched both legs forward until they were almost touching Zeke's desk in front of him.

Across the aisle, Gabriella turned to glance at him. He shot her a smile, then returned his attention to his feet.

Okay, what was that first exercise again? He thought back, trying to picture exactly what the doctor had showed him. Bad foot on the floor, he remembered. Then put the ankle of my good foot on top of the bad one.

He did so. His injured ankle throbbed a bit, but he ignored the pain.

Okay, now press down with the good heel and try to lift with the bad foot, he thought. One, two, three . . .

"Ow!" he shouted, startled by a sudden sharp pain stabbing through his injured ankle.

"Mr. Bolton!" The drama teacher spun around and glared at him. "Did you have something to add to our discussion of ancient Greek tragedy?"

Troy bit his lip, carefully returning both his feet to the floor as the pain subsided to a dull throb. "Sorry, Ms. Darbus," he said. "It won't happen again."

Across the way, Gabriella watched worriedly as Troy slumped down in his seat again. She had already guessed what he was doing—he'd told her about the ankle exercises his doctor had assigned him. But she wasn't quite sure what had inspired him to do them in class.

I hope he's okay, she thought. He seems really depressed about this whole injury thing.

Gabriella understood why he was so upset—that winning streak was a big deal. But she wished he could just step back and see the big picture. So what if he missed a game or two? So what if the streak ended this weekend? The sprain was just an accident—it could have happened to anybody. It wasn't his fault.

Realizing that she'd totally missed the last five minutes of Ms. Darbus's lecture, she sighed, tore her gaze away from Troy, and turned to face the front again. As she did, she caught Ashley glancing at her from the next row. Ashley looked over at Troy, then shrugged and shot Gabriella a sympathetic smile.

Gabriella smiled back, suddenly feeling a little bit better about the situation. It was always nice to know that someone else understood. Now if only she could share some of those warm, hopeful feelings with Troy . . .

CHAPTER SIX

Troy tapped his good foot on the bleacher below him as he watched the rest of the Wildcats race down the court. The tapping shook the bench, which made his bad ankle throb, but he barely noticed. He was totally focused on the action out on the floor. Practice had begun half an hour earlier, and after some warm-up drills, the coach was having the guys run practice plays.

"Heads up, Chad," Troy muttered under his breath as he watched his teammates drive for the basket. "You're letting Zeke get away from you."

On the sidelines, his father blew his whistle sharply. "Danforth!" Coach Bolton barked. "I thought I told you to cover Zeke. How are you going to do that from ten yards behind him?"

"I'll keep trying." Chad bent over and rested his hands on his knees, breathing hard. "But he's got longer legs than me."

Troy couldn't resist. "Try going left instead of shadowing him the regular way!" he called out to Chad. "That way it doesn't matter who's faster—you'll be able to cut him off either way."

Chad flashed him a grin. "Hey, you got it, Coach!" he joked, as he straightened up and grabbed the ball from Zeke.

Coach Bolton glanced at Troy and nodded slightly. "Yes, good call," he said approvingly.

At that moment, the school secretary appeared in the gym doorway. "Coach Bolton," she said. "There's a phone call for you in the office. Something about the team's schedule for next month."

"I'll be right there. Okay, guys, I'll be back shortly," the coach said. He winked proudly at Troy. "In the meantime, Assistant Coach Bolton can take over for me."

He jogged off the court toward the office. The Wildcats all relaxed as soon as he was gone. Zeke stole the ball back from Chad and tossed it at the basket, while Chad dropped to the floor and stretched out on his back. Some of the guys wandered off the court to get their water bottles and others sat on the bench, taking a breather.

"Hey, what are you guys doing?" Troy called out, scooting down to the lowest bleacher. "Didn't you hear what Coach said? I can take over until he gets back. It's not like I'm doing anything else up here."

"I'm pretty sure the coach was just kidding," Zeke said. "It's time for a break anyway."

"We don't have time for breaks." Troy's mind was already filled with ideas for ways the team could improve. "Not if we want to keep that streak alive this weekend. Jefferson is tough, and they'll be ready for us. We've got to be just as ready for them. So let's start with some free-throw drills, okay?"

"Give it up, Troy," Chad said from the floor. "Your dad will be back in a second."

Troy frowned. "But why waste time when we could be getting better?"

"We?" Jason grumbled, shooting a pointed look at Troy's ankle splint.

"Yes, *we*," Troy said. "We're a team. And last I checked, I'm still the team captain, right?"

Chad groaned and climbed to his feet. "Fine," he said, sounding a little grumpy. "What do you want us to do, Oh Great Assistant Coach and Team Captain?" He swept down into a dramatic bow.

Troy could tell Chad was annoyed, but he ignored the attitude. He'll thank me this weekend when we're celebrating victory number ten, he told himself.

"Let's try this," he said, rubbing his hands together and scanning the team. "Line up on the free-throw line. We'll start with that drill where you take turns shooting, rebounding, and then passing. Do you remember?" When the team nodded and started moving into position, Troy continued. "That way you can all get sharper on the free throws, especially Jason and Ricky. It will also give Brad and Mike a chance to improve their passing skills, and of course Zeke can use some help with rebounds."

Zeke looked startled. "Hey, my rebounds aren't that bad," he protested. "Are they?"

"You heard the coach." Chad rolled his eyes, grabbed the ball, and started to dribble. "Let's hustle."

"French fry?" Taylor offered. She held out her plate.

"Thanks." Gabriella took a fry. The Scholastic Decathlon team meeting had just ended, and she and Taylor were at a diner near the school. "I'm starving. Ashley wanted me to help her catch up on her math homework during lunch period, so

I barely had time to eat." She popped the fry into her mouth.

Taylor pursed her lips. "Yes," she said. "Where *is* your shadow this afternoon, anyway?"

"Be nice," Gabriella chided. "I know Ashley's been tagging along a lot. But she only got here yesterday. She doesn't know many people yet."

"Hmm." Taylor didn't look convinced. "That's not how it looks to me. It seems like she's already good pals with most of the basketball team. At least she's taking every chance she gets to hang around them."

Gabriella was a little surprised. Taylor really sounded down on Ashley for some reason. "Well, anyway, I don't know where she is right now," she replied. "She said she had something to do after school today." She cleared her throat. "Look, Taylor. I know she got off on the wrong foot with you by flirting with Chad like that, but—"

"Heads up." Taylor was staring over Gabriella's head, not seeming to have heard what she was saying. "Sharpay sighting, ten o'clock."

Gabriella glanced over her shoulder. Sharpay had just stalked into the diner, her cell phone pressed to her ear and an irritated scowl on her face.

"Yikes," Gabriella whispered, sliding down in her seat. "She doesn't look happy."

Taylor grabbed the menu and shielded her face with it. She peeked around at Gabriella. "Right," she whispered back. "And an unhappy Sharpay is a Sharpay to be avoided."

"Shut up and listen to me, Ryan!" Sharpay squawked into her phone, earning stares from the other customers. "I don't care how far behind you are in English class. You need to get over to that country club *today* and make sure the stage is up to par. Oh, and while you're there, you must insist that they let you taste the canapés. That incompetent chef claimed not to have any prepared when I stopped in before school today. Oh, and one more thing . . ."

Taylor leaned across the table, still hidden behind the menu. "Sounds like the big rock-star-party plans aren't going too smoothly," she murmured to Gabriella.

Gabriella nodded. "I'm sure Sharpay will pull it off somehow, though," she whispered back. "She always does."

". . . and if you kind of spin the ball a little, I think you'll find it really helps . . ." Troy swung his crutches faster, trying to keep up with Jason on the way out of the gym. "Hey, slow down, man. I'm down to one good leg here, remember?"

"Sorry, Troy," Jason said.

"Troy! There you are!"

Troy glanced over and saw Ashley hurrying toward him. "Oh. Hello," he greeted her, wondering what she was doing there. Practice had run pretty late, and he was sure all the other school clubs had long since wrapped up their meetings or rehearsals. "What's up?"

"I just came by to see how practice went." She

smiled. "I'm really looking forward to seeing you guys play on Saturday."

"Practice was great," Troy said. "Um, Jason and I were just going over some stuff, so we'd better—"

"Actually, I've got to go," Jason interrupted. "I forgot, I'm supposed to babysit my little brother tonight. Catch you tomorrow, Troy."

"Oh. Okay. See you later." Troy was a little disappointed. Still, he figured he could continue the conversation with Jason tomorrow.

Ashley looked pleased by Jason's departure. "Cool," she said. "Now you totally have time to tell me all about how your leg's doing."

"Not too bad," Troy said. "The splint helps."

"Awesome," Ashley said. "I guess that means you might even be feeling well enough to dance to Trina's music at Sharpay's party Saturday night, huh?"

"What? Oh—maybe," Troy said, still distracted by his thoughts about the practice that had just ended.

"That party sounds like it's going to be so cool," Ashley went on. "I really wish I could go. But I doubt Sharpay will invite a newbie like me, right?"

"Right," Troy said. Suddenly realizing what she'd just said, he cleared his throat. "Er, I mean no. She might invite you, Ashley." He laughed. "Sharpay can be—hard to predict."

"Wow, that would be so awesome if I got to go! But I'm still not getting my hopes up too high." Ashley tilted her head and smiled at him. "But you'll be there for sure, right, Troy?"

Troy barely heard her. His mind was still back in the gym. At first, he'd feared his injury meant he had nothing to contribute to the team. But after today's practice, he realized he'd been all wrong. Maybe he couldn't actually play against Jefferson, but he could help in other ways. After all, who knew the Wildcats—their strengths, their weaknesses—better than him? With his extra coaching, the team would be better than ever!

Realizing that Ashley was gazing at him expectantly, he searched his mind for what she'd just said. Oh, right—Sharpay's party.

"Sure, I'll be there, I guess," he said. "Especially if—no, *when*—we win the game that day." He smiled, picturing the way his teammates would carry him onto the court to share in the victory. "We'll all want to celebrate."

CHAPTER SEVEN

"**W**here's your new friend this morning?" Taylor asked the next day as she and Gabriella headed for homeroom. "I thought she'd be waiting for you in the lobby again."

Gabriella shrugged. After the Sharpay sighting the previous afternoon, she and Taylor had spent the rest of their time together discussing the party and Trina Chica. They'd never returned to the topic of Ashley.

I guess Taylor just doesn't appreciate Ashley

the way I do, Gabriella thought. At least not yet. Maybe I can help her come around. After all, just because Ashley is never going to be Scholastic Decathlon Girl, it doesn't mean we can't be friends with her.

"I'm not sure where she is," she told Taylor. "I guess we'll see her in homeroom."

"I guess you're ri—" Taylor's voice trailed off. They'd just reached the classroom doorway, and she was staring through it.

Gabriella followed her gaze and saw Ashley perched on the edge of Sharpay's desk. She was giggling and chattering rapidly at Sharpay and Ryan.

As she entered with Taylor, Gabriella could hear what Ashley was saying. ". . . and that necklace is superamazing, too. Sharpay, where did you get your awesome sense of fashion?"

Sharpay smirked and adjusted the fur-trimmed collar of her top. "Some of us are just born with it."

Taylor rolled her eyes. "I guess it shouldn't be a surprise to see Ashley hanging all over Sharpay," she commented. "After all, the whole school is going crazy over this party."

Gabriella knew that was true. Ever since her big announcement, Sharpay had been the center of attention.

"Excuse me, Ashley," Sharpay said loudly, fluttering one hand. "This little chat has been fun. But if you could give me a moment, I urgently need to discuss some important party plans with my brother."

"Sure, Sharpay. I'll see you later." Ashley hopped down off the desk. She spotted Gabriella and Taylor heading to their seats and hurried over. "Guess what Sharpay just told me?" she exclaimed excitedly. "She's planning to have the ice sculpture done in the shape of Trina Chica. Isn't that cool?"

"Yes," Taylor said. "Literally."

"I know!" Ashley didn't seem to notice Taylor's joke. "And there's going to be this awesome DJ before Trina's show, and some of the appetizers will have real caviar in them, and the decorations will all be pink and lavender to match the flower arrangements, and—"

"That's nice, Ashley," Gabriella said, setting her bag down on her desk. "Sharpay never does anything halfway."

Ashley clasped her hands and sighed. "I know I'm brand-new, and it's totally a long shot," she said. "Especially since Sharpay says the guest list will be *very* exclusive. But I just think it would be so supercool to go to that party and see Trina Chica and hang out with you guys and Troy and the whole gang. . . ."

Gabriella shrugged. "I'm not sure if Troy is even planning to go. His leg might not be up to partying by then."

"Oh, he's *definitely* going!" Ashley assured her. "He told me so himself."

"He did? When?" Gabriella asked.

"Yesterday after basketball practice." Ashley's eyes suddenly widened. "Oh! I'll be right back—

I forgot to tell Sharpay I saw those shoes she was wearing yesterday on TV."

She hurried off. Taylor turned and raised an eyebrow at Gabriella.

"So Ashley was chatting with Troy after basketball practice, hmm?" she said. "Sounds like *that's* what she had to do after school yesterday."

"Oh, come on." Gabriella had to admit it was a little strange. But she was sure there was a reasonable explanation. Wasn't there? "Maybe she just ran into him on the way out or something. I told you—she's just trying to fit in and make friends."

When sixth period ended, Troy headed out into the hallway as quickly as his crutches would allow. He spotted Mike Brown, one of his teammates, at the water fountain.

"Yo, Brown!" he called. "Just who I wanted to see."

Mike glanced up. "Oh. Troy. Hi."

"Hey." Troy gave him a friendly smile.

"Listen, I was thinking about something during English class. You know how you've been having so much trouble with your jump shots the last few games? I came up with a great idea to help you."

"Really?" Mike glanced over his shoulder. "That's great. But listen, I really need to run to my locker. I, uh, forgot my math book. I'll catch you later, okay?"

"Oh. Okay." Troy, who was a little disappointed, shrugged as Mike disappeared into the crowd. This was the second time he had brushed him off before he could explain his idea—the first time, at lunch, Mike had spilled soda all over himself and left to change clothes. Troy was starting to wonder if he was focused enough on what the team needed to accomplish before that weekend's game.

Just then, Troy spotted Jason walking down the hall. He smiled. He'd been looking for him all day, but this was the first time he'd seen him outside of class.

"Hey, Jason!" he called, swinging his crutches into gear again. "Wait up. I need to talk to you about your passing. . . ."

Gabriella stood up and quickly gathered her things. Peer tutoring had run a little long, and she checked her watch, wondering if she still had time to drop in on the end of the Scholastic Decathlon meeting.

Still looking down at her watch, she almost collided with Sharpay and Ryan in the doorway. "Easy, Gabriella!" Sharpay cried, holding up her arm defensively. "If you're that eager to talk to me, just ask."

"What? Oh, no, I wasn't—" Gabriella began.

But she could tell Sharpay wasn't listening. "Of course, you're not the only one chasing me down these days. Right, Ryan?"

"Right," Ryan agreed. "Especially now that you've almost finished your guest list."

"Hush!" Sharpay looked alarmed. "You're not supposed to just go around blurting out big news like that! It could cause a riot." Her expression relaxed. "But I'm sure Gabriella won't spill our little secret. Right, Gabriella?" She winked. "Especially since there's a pretty good chance your name might just possibly be on that list. Oh, and Troy's, too, of course, and the rest of your little gang."

"Oh. Um, that's cool." Gabriella did her best to sound properly honored. "The party sounds like fun, Sharpay. I love Trina Chica."

"Well, there are a few people I haven't quite decided about yet." Sharpay stroked her chin thoughtfully. "Your new friend Ashley, for instance. On the one hand, she has excellent taste in fashion. On the other, she seems a little too . . . hmm . . . *desperate*, somehow. Know what I mean?"

"Oh, yes." Ryan nodded. "Totally desperate."

"Of course," Sharpay continued, "if you and Troy really want her to be invited, I might be able to overlook Ashley's less-than-A-list qualities. . . ."

Gabriella hesitated. Despite what she'd said to Taylor earlier, she couldn't stop thinking about how Ashley had fibbed the day before. Or had she?

What difference does it make, really? Gabriella told herself. So maybe she wanted to hang around and talk to the basketball guys, or maybe it was just a coincidence that she ran into Troy. It's not a big deal, either way. And I know how much an invitation to Sharpay's party would mean to Ashley. How can I mess that up for her?

"Sure," she told Sharpay. "I'd totally owe you one."

"I see." Sharpay smiled. "Well, I can't commit to anything, but I'll certainly take your recommendation under advisement."

"Thanks," Gabriella said. "I know Ashley will appreciate that."

CHAPTER EIGHT

"**O**ops!" Ashley stopped short just outside of homeroom. "I forgot my English book. I'd better go get it."

"Okay," Gabriella said. "See you in a minute."

She walked into the classroom as Ashley hurried off in the opposite direction. It was Thursday morning, and the bell wasn't due to ring for twenty minutes. Most of the students were still at their lockers or hanging out in the lobby or cafeteria. But Gabriella wanted to get to homeroom early so she would have a chance to check over her math homework.

Troy was there early, too. He was leaning on his crutches in front of Chad's desk, talking to Chad earnestly.

". . . and I really think if you try it my way, you'll get it," he was saying as Gabriella approached. "It should really help you improve your shooting."

Gabriella couldn't help noticing that Chad looked rather exasperated as he answered. "Yeah," he said. "Guess I didn't realize how much my shooting stinks until you pointed it out. Thanks a lot, bro."

"Hey, don't be too hard on yourself," Troy said with a smile. "And listen, if you want me to talk you through it during free period, I'd be glad to—"

"Hi," Gabriella interrupted. "You guys are here early."

Troy jumped, a little startled. He'd been so

focused on talking to Chad that he hadn't noticed Gabriella enter. But he was even happier than usual to see her. As devoted as he was to helping the team get better before Saturday's game, he realized he needed to talk to her about something important, too.

It's amazing how much I notice now that I'm not focused on my own playing, he thought. It's like there's all this stuff going on that I never would've paid much attention to before.

"Hey, Gabriella," he said. "Yeah, I got here early to talk to the guys about a few new ideas I had. The game's only two days away, and we still have a lot of work to do. But now that you're here, I really need to talk to you about someth—"

"Yo, Gabriella's right!" Chad interrupted. "It's totally early. I can't be seen getting to homeroom this early, or it might ruin my cool slacker reputation. See you ten seconds before the bell, man." Without waiting for a response, he dashed for the classroom door. He was in such a hurry that he left his basketball behind.

"Okay!" Troy called after him. "We can finish our talk later."

Gabriella sat down at the empty desk across from Troy. "So what did you want to talk to me about?" she asked. "Is it about Sharpay's party?" She smiled and rolled her eyes. "She pretty much told me we're both invited."

"It's not about that." Troy shook his head, glanced at the door, and lowered his voice. "Actually, it's about Ashley."

"What about her?" Gabriella asked.

Troy took a deep breath. "I was trying to be nice to her," he said. "Help her fit in, like you've been doing. But I had a chance to talk to her after practice the other day, and I've had a lot of extra time to pay attention lately. . . ." He waved a hand at his sprained ankle.

"So what are you saying, Troy?" Gabriella asked with a little frown.

"I'm saying be careful." Troy leaned closer,

gazing at her solemnly. "I'm not sure she's sincere—you know, about being friends with you."

"What?" Gabriella's frown grew deeper. "Why would you say something like that? Did she say something bad about me?"

"No, nothing like that. Just call it a hunch," Troy said. "She's not your kind of person."

"Oh." Gabriella looked perplexed. "Well, I don't know. I mean, I know that Ashley and I don't have that much in common, and it's kind of weird how she's so impressed by Sharpay. But I'm not sure it's fair to judge what kind of person she is while she's still adjusting to a new school and everything. . . ."

"You know what your problem is, Gabriella?" Troy said. "You're too nice. You did your duty by showing her around for the first few days. Why not leave it at that?"

"You don't understand," Gabriella protested. "You've always gone to school here, Troy— you don't know what it's like to be the new kid and try to fit in with a bunch of people who have known each other for years."

"Maybe not. But I really think you ought to stop spending so much time with Ashley. It's for your own good."

"Oh, really?" Gabriella's eyes flashed. "Look, you don't need to start bossing me around like you've been doing with your teammates."

"What?" Troy recoiled, as startled as if she'd just slapped him. "I haven't been bossing anyone around!"

"I know—I'm sorry," Gabriella said immediately, her expression softening. "That just slipped out—what you said really reminded me how miserable it can be to be the new kid."

"I'm not bossing anyone around," Troy repeated, still a little astounded that she would say such a thing. "I mean, sure, I'm giving a few of the guys some pointers. But that's only because I'm trying to help out any way I can, to make up for being injured."

"Of course," Gabriella said with an apologetic smile. She reached over and touched his hand.

"I'm sure the guys appreciate your concern. Just like I do."

"Thanks." He smiled back briefly. "They know I'm just trying to help."

Don't they? he added silently, biting his lip and glancing down at Chad's basketball.

"Hey, everyone!" Ashley cried, bursting in through the classroom door. "Come quick! Sharpay's about to give out her party invitations!"

The few other students in the room jumped up and rushed for the door. Gabriella hopped out of her chair. "Come on," she said to Troy. "Let's go see."

As Troy started gathering his crutches, she hurried out of the room after Ashley, who was racing down the hall at top speed. Normally Gabriella wouldn't care that much about Sharpay's big announcement, but she needed a moment away from Troy to clear her mind. She could tell that what she'd just blurted out had hurt his feelings.

It's kind of true, though, she told herself as she joined the stream of students pouring toward the lobby. Like the way he was with Chad just now. And I've seen the looks some of the other guys have been giving him lately. I know he's trying to help; I'm just not sure they see it that way. . . .

She glanced over her shoulder and saw Troy hobbling along a few yards behind. "Hey, wait up!" he called to her.

She hurried back to join him. "Sorry," she said. "Guess I was just excited to see whether I made the cut."

"I think we're about to find out."

Sharpay and Ryan were standing in front of the trophy case. Dozens of students were gathered around them, jostling for position.

"Ladies and gentlemen!" Sharpay announced, her stage-trained voice carrying over the din of her eager audience. "Thanks for coming. I'm afraid for most of you, this is going to be bad news. As you all know, Trina Chica will be appearing at my party, and that means the guest list must be limited to the truly elite—that is, approximately fifty of my closest and dearest friends."

"Just spill it, Sharpay!" called out someone who sounded like Chad. "Who's invited?"

Sharpay frowned. "All right, all right," she said. "Ryan?"

She held out her hand. Ryan pulled a stack of pink and lavender envelopes out of his backpack and handed them over.

"If I call your name, please come forward in an orderly fashion," Sharpay said. She glanced down at the first envelope. "Troy Bolton . . . Zeke Baylor . . . Gabriella Montez . . ."

It took Sharpay several minutes to read through all the names. In addition to Troy and Gabriella, she'd invited the entire basketball team, all of the drama club, most of the cheerleaders, and a few others, including Taylor and a couple of Gabriella's other friends. Finally, she was down to one remaining envelope.

"And finally, the last invitee." She paused dramatically and glanced around. "It goes to— Ashley Appleton."

"Omigosh!" Ashley shrieked. She pushed forward, grabbing the invitation eagerly. "Thank you so much, Sharpay! I can't believe it!"

"You're welcome." Sharpay flashed her a smile. Then she shrugged. "As for the rest of you—I'm sorry. We can't all be part of the 'in' crowd."

There was a murmur of annoyance from the people who hadn't been invited. Gabriella could hear a lot of people complaining about missing the chance to see Trina Chica. Sharpay didn't stick around to listen—she and Ryan hurried off down the hall toward homeroom without a backward glance.

"Isn't this awesome?" Ashley squealed, racing over and throwing herself at Gabriella. She jumped up and down excitedly, hugging Gabriella tightly. "We're going to have so much fun!"

Gabriella laughed, unable to answer—Ashley was squeezing her too hard. She couldn't resist sneaking a slightly smug told-you-so glance at Troy as she hugged Ashley back.

CHAPTER NINE

"What team?" Chad shouted.

"Wildcats!" the rest of the team yelled back.

"Getcha head in the game!" Chad howled.

Troy joined in the cheer with everyone else. But the shouts were still echoing off the locker-room walls when he held up a hand for attention. The game was scheduled to start in a few minutes. There was still a lot to accomplish before then.

"Listen, guys," he said, leaning forward on

his crutches. "Let's talk tactics for a second."

"Forget that stuff, man." Jason grinned. "We're ready to totally slay Jefferson! What do you say, guys—think we'll win by thirty points?"

"Fifty!" Zeke cried, pumping his fist in the air.

"No way!" Chad shouted. "Eighty!"

Troy smiled. He was glad to see that the team was pumped up and ready to win. That was great. But he was still a little worried—it was the first time in a while that they'd had to play a tough opponent without one of their usual starters, and the first time in years since Troy had missed an important game. His father had stepped out of the locker room for a few minutes, so it was up to him to get them focused on exactly what they had to do today.

"Okay, okay," he said. "But we really should go over a few last-minute strategies. Like Jason, make sure you keep the pressure on their offense. Mike, keep looking for the pass from downcourt—don't lose focus. And Zeke, you've got to remember those tips I gave you for when you go for the rebound, and—"

"Enough!" Chad shouted, slamming his hand down on the bench. "Give it a rest, man!"

"What?" Troy was so startled he took a step backward and almost tripped over his crutches. "What do you mean?"

"He's right." Jason shrugged apologetically. "Sorry, Troy. But the busybody stuff is getting old, you know?"

Zeke nodded. "We all feel bad about your ankle. But you've got to chill."

"Yeah! You're driving us all nuts!" Mike cried.

Troy put a hand to his head. "Are you kidding me?" he exclaimed.

He stared from one serious face to another. He couldn't believe the team was turning on him like this, especially right before the game. Couldn't they see he was just trying to help them?

"Excuse me," he mumbled. "I think I'd better get out of your hair now. I wouldn't want to be a busybody or anything." He turned and hobbled out of the locker room as fast as he could.

"Troy, wait!" Zeke called.

"Come on, bro," Chad added. "We were just—"

But Troy didn't hear the rest. He let the locker-room door slam shut behind him.

In the distance, he could hear the muffled sounds of chanting and cheering from the gym. He could picture the scene, because he'd seen it dozens of times before—the cheerleaders would be doing their thing, getting the crowd pumped up. On the opposite side of the floor, the visiting team's fans would be waving their banners and trying in vain to outshout the home-team fans.

But back here in the hallway outside the locker room, it was quiet and empty. That matched Troy's mood perfectly.

How could they be so ungrateful? he thought as he swung down the hall. It's bad enough I let them down by getting hurt. They should know that I'm just tring to make up for that by helping them out in the only way I can. . . .

The thought drifted off as he heard the sound of girls' voices around the corner just ahead. He grimaced as he realized one of them belonged to Sharpay. Stopping short, he did his best to turn around without letting the tips of his crutches squeak against the floor. The last thing he needed right now was to encounter Sharpay. He wasn't sure he could pretend to be interested in her big party when he was so distracted by what had just happened.

". . . and so when Gabriella said how much she wanted you to come—practically begged me to invite you!—I wasn't sure what to do. I mean, of course I was planning to invite Gabriella herself, but I really wanted to limit the number of her little Einsteinesque friends. . . ."

Troy stopped short again. He tilted his head, curious. Why was Sharpay talking about Gabriella? And who was the other girl?

His eyes widened as he recognized the second voice. It was Ashley.

"Oh, I understand completely." Ashley let out a short laugh. "But don't worry, I'm not like that at all, Sharpay. Actually, I'm not even that close with Gabriella. The principal wanted me to let her show me around, so I did."

"Well, okay," Sharpay said. "I just couldn't imagine what someone with your obvious taste in fashion would have in common with someone like Gabriella. I mean, have you *seen* the way she dresses?"

"I know!" Ashley laughed again. "She's nice and all, but I don't think she'd know a designer label unless it was in one of those chemistry equations she loves so much. Anyway, Sharpay, thanks again for inviting me. And like I said, if you need any more help getting ready tonight . . ."

"Now that you mention it, why don't you come to the country club an hour early?" Sharpay said. "I'm sure Ryan would appreciate some help setting up. He's sort of in charge of the operational details."

"Sure!" Ashley said eagerly. "I'll totally be there, Sharpay. I'm awesome at operational details."

Troy backed away as quickly as he could on his crutches. His mind was spinning. He'd suspected that Ashley was bad news, but now he knew it for sure. She was almost making it sound as if *she* had been doing *Gabriella* a favor by hanging around her all week!

I tried to tell her, Troy thought, shaking his head. He shot a look toward the locker room. But it seems like nobody wants to listen to me these days. . . .

He thought back to his conversation with Gabriella on Thursday. Sharpay's big invitation presentation had interrupted them before he could really talk about his concerns, and after that, both of them had let it drop. It just hadn't seemed worth arguing over.

But now things were different. I've got to go out there and tell her what I just heard, Troy thought grimly, swinging his crutches in the direction of the gym entrance. *She needs to know the truth.*

"Go Wildcats! Whooo!" Gabriella cheered along with the crowd. She grinned at Taylor. "The cheerleaders look really good today, don't they?"

Taylor didn't seem to be listening. "Here comes your new best friend," she muttered.

Gabriella glanced down and saw Ashley climbing up the stands toward them. "Hey," she said breathlessly, plopping down on the bench beside Gabriella. "I didn't miss anything, did I?"

"The game should be starting any second now," Gabriella said. "You got here just in time. What took you so long, anyway?"

"Oh, there was a line in the bathroom," Ashley lied. "So, are you guys totally psyched about the party tonight? I can't believe we're actually going to see Trina Chica live!"

Even Taylor looked excited about that. "I know," she said. "Looks like Sharpay really pulled it off this time."

"Gabriella! Hey—there you are!"

This time when Gabriella glanced down, she saw Troy clambering over the bleachers, dragging his crutches. "Be careful!" she called to him. "I thought you were supposed to keep your weight off your bad ankle."

"Never mind that." Troy hopped up the last couple of steps on one foot. "Gabriella, I really need to talk to you. *Privately.*" He shot a glance at the other two girls. "It's kind of important."

"AND NOW," the PA system suddenly blared out, "INTRODUCING YOUR EAST. HIGH WILDCATS!"

A roar of enthusiasm rose from the fans all around them. Down on the floor, the team jogged out from the direction of the locker room, pumping their fists and waving to the crowd. The cheerleaders went wild, shaking their pom-poms and doing cartwheels on the sidelines.

Gabriella smiled helplessly at Troy. "Can it wait?" she asked, doing her best to make herself heard over the screams of the fans.

Troy's shoulders slumped. "Guess it'll have to," he said. He turned around and started making his way back down toward the bench to rejoin the team.

CHAPTER TEN

"**H**ave fun tonight, Troy." Troy's father pulled his car to the curb outside the country club. "And tell the guys to celebrate big. They played a heck of a game today." He reached over and punched Troy lightly on the arm. "Even without their team captain out on the floor."

Troy forced a smile. "I'll tell them, Dad." He undid his seat belt. "Thanks for the ride."

He knew his father was proud of the Wildcats. They'd kept the winning streak alive, beating Jefferson by almost twenty points.

Troy was happy about that, too. But he was still smarting a little from the confrontation with his teammates before the game. Although he'd sat on the bench with them, he hadn't really had a chance to talk to anyone about what had happened in the locker room. Some of the guys on the bench had made a point to high-five him after each score, which told Troy they felt bad about the whole scene and were trying to pretend it hadn't happened. But he wasn't quite ready to forget.

I'll have to deal with that tonight, he told himself as he opened the car door and climbed out with the help of his crutches. But first I want to find Gabriella and warn her about Ashley.

That was another conversation he hadn't had time for at the game. Things had been too crazy at halftime, and she had left right after the buzzer, promising to meet him at the party.

Troy waved as his father pulled away, then turned to head into the country club. There were quite a few East High students milling around outside. "Yo, Bolton!" a skateboarder shouted, giving Troy a thumbs-up. "Awesome game today, dude."

"Thanks," Troy called back. "Not that I had anything to do with it," he muttered to himself.

"Sure you did, Troy," someone said from right behind him.

Troy spun around. "Guys!" he said, seeing the entire basketball team standing there. They looked much different than they had earlier. For one thing, they had changed out of their bright red Wildcats uniforms and were dressed up to party. For another, they looked somber rather than excited and triumphant, as he'd last seen them.

"We've been waiting for you, man," Chad said, stepping forward.

"Yeah." Jason stepped up beside him. "We want to apologize. We acted like real jerks to you before the game."

"We know you were only trying to help us win," Zeke added.

Suddenly Troy felt as if a huge weight had been lifted off his shoulders. "Thanks, guys," he said, his face relaxing into a smile. "And you're right—I *was* just trying to help."

Zeke nodded. "Like when you kept telling me how much my rebounds stunk? It made me want to get better."

"Your rebounds don't stink," Troy protested. "I just had some ideas to help you out, that's all."

"Well, I never realized how completely horrible my passing was until you kept telling me, Troy," Mike spoke up. "Maybe if I can get better at that, Coach will let me start more often."

Troy shot him a thumbs-up, but he was a little taken aback by Mike's comment. He didn't remember telling Mike that his passing skills were *horrible*, exactly. . . .

"Anyway, we should have been more understanding." Chad grinned. "I mean, we know you must be a little off your game when you start acting like Ms. Darbus directing a play or something."

Troy smiled back weakly. Had he really been *that* bad?

Yeah, he admitted to himself, I guess I was.

"Look, guys," he said, "I'm starting to think *I'm* the one who should be apologizing to all of you. I was trying to be helpful—you know, make up for being on the injured list. I guess maybe I took it a little too far." He gazed around at his teammates. "I didn't mean to make anyone feel bad or whatever. No matter what I said this week, I think you guys are all awesome players, and I'm proud to be part of this team."

Chad lifted his fist to his eye, pretending to wipe away a tear. "That's beautiful, man," he said with a mock sob.

"Whatever, Danforth," Troy said, smiling. "I mean it. I'm sorry I was such a pain all week. It won't happen again."

"You bet it won't," Chad teased. "Because once that ankle is healed, you'd better not ever get injured again!"

"At least not before the end of the season," Zeke added.

That made everyone laugh, including Troy. "It's a deal," he said, high-fiving the others one by one.

"What team?" Chad shouted.

"Wildcats!" Troy cried along with the rest of the team. "Come on, let's go inside and celebrate!"

A few minutes later, Gabriella hurried toward the door to the country club. "Wow," she said. "There sure are a lot of people here."

There had to be at least fifty or sixty students milling around outside. "Hey, Gabriella!" called a girl named Martha Cox, who was a member of the Scholastic Decathlon team. "Do you have an invitation?"

"Uh-huh." Gabriella held up her envelope. "Do you?"

"No—and I *love* Trina Chica!" Martha cried. "Do you think you can sneak me in? Please?"

"Sorry," Gabriella said. "Sharpay made a big

point of telling us they'd be checking names at the door."

"Did I hear you say you have an invitation?" A boy Gabriella didn't know pushed Martha aside and rushed over. He was wearing a Trina Chica T-shirt, and his expression was wild and desperate. "I'll give you ten bucks for it!"

Gabriella laughed uncertainly and backed away a few steps. "I don't think that will work," she said. "You don't look much like a Gabriella."

"Okay, you win—fifteen bucks! Twenty!"

Gabriella shook her head and kept backing up. "Sorry."

"Twenty-three dollars! No, twenty-five!" the boy howled as she turned and made a break for the door. "Please!"

She was relieved when the doorman ushered her inside away from all the crazed Trina fans. It was a lot quieter in the country-club lobby, though she could hear music, talking, and laughter from the direction of the ballroom.

Gabriella had just started heading that way

when someone raced across the lobby and almost crashed into her. "Whoa!" she exclaimed, jumping back just in time. "Um—Ryan? Are you okay?"

Sharpay's brother skidded to a stop and put both hands to his head. "No, I am not okay!" he cried. "This party is a disaster!"

"What do you mean?" Gabriella asked.

Ryan's left eye was twitching, and his mouth was twisted into a grimace. "I mean *everything* is going wrong. *Everything!*"

Gabriella took a few steps toward the ball-room. Ryan was always a little eccentric, but he definitely seemed more high-strung than usual. "I'm sure it's not that bad," she said.

"Not that bad?" Ryan threw both hands in the air. "Do you have any idea how much is involved in throwing a party of this magnitude? And Sharpay has been so busy talking it up to people—public relations, she calls it—" He rolled his eyes. "—that she dumped all the prep work on me. She should know me better than that—I just can't handle this kind of pressure!"

"Oh, come on. I'm sure you're overreacting. . . ." Gabriella's voice trailed off as she reached the ballroom door and looked inside. The first thing that greeted her was an enormous ice sculpture shaped like a giant chicken. "Wow," she said. "That's . . . interesting."

Ryan choked back a sob. "It was supposed to look like Trina Chica," he said. "I guess the guy heard me wrong. And don't even get me started on the decorations. . . . I told them it was a birthday party, but I think they got us mixed up with someone else. They don't even have the right kind of cake!"

Gabriella glanced around the room. The walls were covered in streamers and balloons in shades of blue and silver. A big banner over the stage at one end of the room read HAPPY 50TH ANNIVERSARY, GRACIE AND BOB!

"Oops," Gabriella said. She couldn't begin to imagine Sharpay's reaction when she first saw that. "Well, I'm sure you did your best, Ryan. . . ."

Just then Ashley raced over to them. She was holding a tray full of blue plastic flatware and mini hot dogs.

"Gabriella! I'm so glad you could make it." Ashley shot her a quick smile. "Come in and enjoy yourself. Sharpay will be along soon—she and I are just taking care of some last minute details that got a little, er . . . messed up." She glared at Ryan, then rushed off again.

Ryan barely seemed to notice Ashley. He was wringing his hands and staring at the "Happy Anniversary" banner in despair. "I don't think half these people are even invited," he moaned. "Sharpay will probably blame me for that, too— once she gets done blaming me for the ice sculpture and the decorations and the missing flowers and the weird appetizers—"

"Well, never mind," Gabriella said, trying to cheer him up. "Nobody will care about any of that stuff once Trina Chica gets here. All they'll remember about this party is that they got to see her sing live, right?"

Ryan let out a strangled little whimper. "But that's the worst part!" he cried. He glanced around to make sure nobody else was listening. "Sharpay kind of fudged that announcement about Trina Chica. See, our father just arranged to link in to the broadcast of the live concert she's doing tonight in Houston."

"Houston?" Gabriella repeated, not quite understanding.

"Yes, Houston," Ryan said. "Trina Chica's not actually coming to the party in person at all."

CHAPTER ELEVEN

"I'll be back," Troy said to his teammates, who were grabbing food off the buffet table.

He'd just spotted Gabriella over near the door talking to Ryan. Popping one last mini hot dog into his mouth, he hurried over as fast as he could on his bad ankle. When he reached Gabriella, her face wore a shocked expression.

"Hey, there you are," Troy greeted her. "You look nice. What's wrong?"

"Nothing!" Ryan cried, his voice almost a

squeak. "Absolutely nothing! And, anyway, it's not my fault!"

He raced away toward the stage. Troy stared after him for a moment, then turned to Gabriella. "What was that all about?"

"Hello, everyone!" Just then, Sharpay stepped onstage with a microphone. Her amplified voice poured out over the crowd along with a whine of feedback. "Welcome to my party."

"I think you're about to find out," Gabriella told Troy with a funny little half-smile.

"Okay." Troy was confused, but he wasn't really that interested. Ryan and Sharpay were always a little odd. Why should tonight be any different? "This is some party, huh? What's with the big ice turkey?"

Gabriella glanced at the ice sculpture. "I think that was a mistake," she said. Her gaze wandered around the room, which was now packed. Kids were jostling each other in front of the stage, while others wolfed down the appetizers on the buffet table. "I'm starting to wonder if the guy checking invitations is making some mistakes, too. It sure looks like there are more people here than Sharpay invited."

"Yeah," Troy agreed. "And that's not even counting everyone outside. Everyone in school is dying to see Trina Chica in person."

Up on the stage, Sharpay was fiddling with her microphone as Ryan watched, looking terrified. Finally she got the feedback under control. "Testing, testing—that's better," she said. "Anyway, welcome to this celebration of the date of my entrance into the world. Oh, and Ryan's too, of course. I'm so glad you all . . ." Her voice faltered for a moment as she looked around the jam-packed ballroom. "Um, that you all are here to share it with me. I mean, us."

"Yo! We want to see Trina!" someone shouted from right in front of the stage.

Sharpay frowned. "As I was saying," she went on, placing one hand dramatically on her heart, "I always find myself in a pensive mood at this time of the year. It is a new beginning for me, an opportunity to reflect upon past achievements and triumphs, and—"

"Tri-na! Tri-na!" the kid down front yelled.

Before long the people around him picked up the chant. Within moments, the entire room echoed with it: *"Tri-na! Tri-na! Tri-na!"*

"Be quiet!" Sharpay yelled, her amplified voice bouncing off the walls. As her audience fell quiet, she glared out at them. "Look, you'll just have to wait a while, okay?"

"But we want Trina!" someone yelled from one side of the large room. Troy couldn't see who had spoken, but it sounded a lot like Chad. "We can listen to you squawk anytime, Sharpay. Where's Trina?"

"Poor Sharpay," Gabriella murmured.

Troy glanced at her. "Oh, come on," he said. "You know she's loving this. She's just milking the moment for even more attention. As usual."

"I think this time might be a little different," Gabriella said.

Meanwhile the Trina chant had started up again, and Sharpay was clutching the microphone tightly. "I'm telling you, all that yelling is not doing anyone any good!" she cried. "You can't see Trina until eight o'clock no matter how loud and obnoxious you are." She pointed to a girl near the front. "Hey, who are you? Did I invite you? Do I even *know* you?"

"Tri-na! Tri-na!" the crowd chanted.

Looking desperate, Sharpay checked her watch. Gabriella glanced at her own and bit her lip. It was only a few minutes to eight. When is she going to admit the truth? she wondered. The longer she waits, the worse this gets.

"Fine!" Sharpay cried. "You want Trina? You've got her. Ladies and gentlemen, I'm thrilled to introduce the princess of pop, the international superstar, Trina Chica!"

The crowd screamed and surged forward. Eager Trina fans stood on tiptoe trying to get a better look. Even Troy took a few steps forward.

"Don't get too excited," Gabriella advised him.

Onstage, a couple of country club employees wheeled a big-screen TV out of the wings. The crowd noise fell off almost immediately.

"Hey!" someone yelled. "What's going on? Where's Trina?"

Sharpay waved a hand at the TV, a fake-looking smile plastered on her face. "Ta-da," she said weakly. "For your viewing pleasure, we're going to have a simulcast of the Trina Chica concert in Houston tonight."

"What?" several people howled. There was a flurry of exclamations and questions.

"Oh, come on!" Sharpay cried. "Now don't tell me you people thought Trina would actually be *here*, did you? *Everyone* knows she's playing sold-out shows in Houston all weekend."

"But you said—" someone began.

"I said she would be *appearing* at my party," Sharpay broke in quickly. "And she will be—on TV. I never said it would be live, in person."

"No way!" the kid down front shouted. "That's totally lame!"

"Yeah!" Chad called out from near the buffet table. "Lame even for you, Sharpay!" A second later a mini hot dog came flying at the stage, almost hitting Sharpay in the head.

Sharpay clenched her fists and turned toward her brother, who appeared to be trying to sink right through the floor. "Ryan, this is all your fault!" she screamed at the top of her lungs as a torrent of mini hot dogs rained down on them. "If you hadn't messed up everything, this party would've been so fabulous that nobody would have even cared if Trina Chica appeared!"

Troy winced as Sharpay's shriek set off feedback in the microphone. "Yikes," he said. "Now I understand why Ryan looked so upset just now."

Gabriella nodded and reached for his hand. "Maybe we should get out of here before the food fight gets any worse," she suggested.

"Good idea," Troy agreed. "I'm pretty sure I

saw some deviled eggs on the buffet. I wouldn't want to get hit with one of those!"

They made their way toward the ballroom door. A few other partygoers were also heading to the exit, looking disappointed. Onstage, Sharpay and Ryan were still yelling at each other. By now Ashley had jumped up there as well and was loudly coming to Sharpay's defense. Chad and a few of the other Wildcats were still winging hot dogs and other appetizers at the stage and at each other. One of the employees had turned on the TV, and on-screen, Trina Chica was dancing out onstage to begin her concert. Some of the partygoers crowded around to watch and sing along. As Gabriella glanced back, one of the mini hot dogs hit the HAPPY 50TH ANNIVERSARY banner and knocked it down—right on Sharpay's head.

"Wow," Gabriella said. "This is definitely going to be a party to remember."

Soon, Troy and Gabriella were out in the quiet hallway. Now that they were alone, Troy was thinking once again about what he wanted to tell her.

"Let's find somewhere private to talk," he suggested.

While they wandered through the lobby, Gabriella told him everything Ryan had confessed to her. By the time they found themselves on a quiet, empty balcony overlooking the tennis courts, Troy was shaking his head with disbelief.

"How in the world did Sharpay think she was going to pull this off?" he asked, leaning on the balcony railing. Even at this distance, he could still hear the cries and shrieks from the ballroom. "I don't envy her right now, that's for sure. She's never going to live this down."

"This is Sharpay we're talking about," Gabriella said, laughing. "She'll figure out a way to come out smelling like a rose—she always does. I just feel sorry for everyone who was so excited about seeing Trina Chica." She glanced back in the direction of the ballroom. "And for people like Ashley, too. She was so thrilled about being invited to this party—I think she really was expecting it to be the party of the century."

Troy gulped and straightened up. "Speaking of Ashley . . ." he began.

"Wait," Gabriella said, turning to face him. She took both his hands in hers and gazed up at him earnestly. "Before you say anything else, I just want to apologize."

"Apologize?" Troy echoed, taken aback. "For what?"

"For getting so snippy when you tried to warn me about Ashley." She smiled. "I know you were only trying to look out for me. And it was really sweet. Thank you." She shrugged. "Anyway, now that Ashley's becoming friends with Sharpay and her crowd, I doubt we'll be hanging out together as often. It's not like we had that much in common anyway."

"Oh." Troy took that in.

Gabriella was still smiling up at him, looking incredibly beautiful in the moonlight. "Okay, so now I've got that off my chest. What did you want to talk to me about?" she asked softly.

Troy smiled back at her. "It was nothing," he said, squeezing her hands. What good would it do to tell her what he'd overheard? It would only hurt her feelings. And he'd done enough of that sort of thing already that week—even if he hadn't meant to. "I just wanted to tell you how cool I think it was for you to show her around all week. It just goes to show you're a really special person. That's all I needed to say."

Something new is on the way!
Look for the next book in the High School
Musical: Stories from East High series . . .

GET YOUR VOTE ON!

By Beth Beechwood and N. B. Grace
Based on the Disney Channel Original Movie
"High School Musical," Written by Peter Barsocchini

Troy Bolton and Sharpay Evans were in a very strange place. They were sitting next to each other in the boardroom near Principal Matsui's office, staring at a group of people whose lips seemed to be moving in slow motion. The people speaking were members of the school board and they were in the middle of a meeting. It was, Troy thought, even more boring than it had sounded earlier that day when Principal Matsui had suggested they attend. Going over budget numbers, approving the hire of an assistant school nurse, scheduling even more teacher in-service days . . . what in the world were they doing here? Unfortunately, Principal Matsui hadn't clued them in.

I can't believe I missed Monday night practice for this, Troy thought.

I can't believe I missed Inside the Actors Studio *for this,* thought Sharpay.

Troy started to jiggle his leg with impatience, causing the whole row of chairs to shake. The Wildcats had a big game coming up and this was not a good time to be observing the bureaucratic process. Principal Matsui, whose seat had begun to vibrate, shot Troy a look. Troy made an apologetic face and immediately stopped bouncing. Sharpay giggled. She loved seeing Mr. Basketball's face go red. It was surprisingly cute.

"Now on to the renovations budget," Mr. Griffith, the head of the board, said. "Mr.

Bolton, Ms. Evans, would you please stand?"

Troy and Sharpay exchanged nervous glances. What could this possibly have to do with them? Reluctantly, they both stood up.

"We have found some money in the budget that will cover the renovation of either the gymnasium or the auditorium," Mr. Griffith said.

Troy's eyes brightened. A new gym? This was great news! If he tripped over that loose floor plank on the way from the bench to the court one more time, he was going to scream.

Sharpay's heart skipped. A revamped auditorium? How fabulous! She imagined a giant sign with her name displayed in lights. One of these days, East High was going to realize what a star they had on their hands—and the installation of a huge, showstopping sign was the first step in making sure that happened.

Their thoughts were interrupted by Mr. Griffith clearing his throat. "Unfortunately, we don't have enough money to renovate both areas. That means we're going to have to make a hard choice."

Troy and Sharpay looked at each other. A hard choice? It seemed pretty obvious to each of them.

"Well, it's great that East High is getting *any* renovations," Troy said diplomatically. Of course, he thought, it's obvious the gym needs to be updated more than the auditorium.

Not to be outdone, Sharpay added cheerfully, "Yes, it's really wonderful! But how will you choose between two such worthy projects?" The choice is actually quite simple, she thought. After all, the auditorium is always filled with the magic of theater, while the gym is always filled with . . . sweaty people.

Troy wanted to roll his eyes at her supersweet tone, but he didn't. After all, he was dying to know, too.

"That's a very good question," Mr. Griffith said with a little glimmer in his eye. "The school board has decided that this decision offers a great opportunity to demonstrate the power of the vote. For that reason, we're going to let the student body choose which area should be renovated. Principal Matsui suggested that you two would be the best people to organize election campaigns and get students excited about participating in the democratic process. Troy—as captain of the basketball team, it seems fitting that you will campaign for the gymnasium. While you, Sharpay, as our resident drama queen, will campaign for the auditorium. You will have one week to fight for your cause, and then there will be a vote."

Sharpay had barely listened after hearing the word "vote." She was already picturing herself delivering the stump speech to end them all. She would be passionate, convincing, and charismatic. So what if there were no babies to kiss, she would kiss the whole ninth grade if she had to—that marquee would be hers!

"Ms. Evans?" Mr. Matsui bumped her elbow lightly to bring her back to the meeting. "Mr. Griffith was speaking to you."

"Oh, sorry, sir!" Sharpay said. "My wheels are already spinning, trying to figure out the very best and most honest way to go about my campaign."

Troy could no longer resist. He rolled his eyes. He knew this was going to be a long, competitive week.

"Well, that's good to hear, young lady," Mr. Griffith praised. "We look forward to seeing how all this will play out. And remember, keep the process clean and fun, and try to get other students involved."

Principal Matsui stood up then and put one hand on Troy's shoulder and another on Sharpay's. "You can count on these two to run fine campaigns, sir," he beamed.

With that, Mr. Griffith adjourned the meeting, and the room rustled with the sound of people putting away papers. But Principal Matsui stopped Troy and Sharpay from leaving. "I hope you intend to keep the antics to a minimum and to make sure that no matter the result, East High comes out looking like the ultimate winner in the end," he said quietly.

Troy and Sharpay nodded. Principal Matsui was always concerned with appearances, and this was an opportunity to really impress the school board. Both Troy and Sharpay understood this.

"Of course, sir," Troy nodded confidently.

"Yes, of course," Sharpay said, before adding, "but the drama club will be the real winner." She raised her eyebrows at Troy. "See you on the campaign trail!" she exclaimed. Then she practically skipped out of the room.

Troy figured that she was running home to tell Ryan the news and that they would then call an emergency late-night meeting of the drama club to get a very early jump on things. At first, this annoyed him. But as he left the boardroom, he realized he'd better do the same if he were going to compete with Sharpay.

He made a beeline for the gym. Practice would be over, but usually the guys hung out in the locker room afterward. Sure enough, when he opened the door, he found his team sitting in the bleachers, going over every detail of practice.

"Hey! How was the big board meeting, Mr. Bolton?" Chad Danforth asked in a mock-serious tone when he saw his best friend walk in. But even as he said it, a wide grin broke out across his face.

"Actually," Troy said, grabbing a seat, "it started out pretty mind-numbing, but I have to say it got extremely interesting later on."

"How could a school-board meeting possibly be interesting?" Zeke Baylor asked, dribbling a ball between his legs.

"Well, as it turns out, there is some money in the budget for a big renovation project, and . . ." Troy paused for dramatic effect, ". . . either the gym or the auditorium will get it."

"Awesome!" Chad said.

"What do you mean 'either'?" Zeke asked.

"Well, that's the thing," Troy explained. "There's going to be a schoolwide vote at the end of the week. We have to run a campaign to get the most votes. Oh, and . . ." he paused before adding, ". . . Sharpay is running the other campaign."

The team all looked at Troy, calculating what this meant.

"We can do this, guys," Troy said, trying to sound encouraging.

"Of course we can—we've got it in the bag. We're the basketball team. But Sharpay is tough competition, Troy," Chad reminded his friend. He did not look thrilled.

"Oh, I know," Troy said. "I'm sure she's already plotting away. She ran out of the meeting in such a hurry, there is no way she and Ryan aren't building a headquarters as we speak."

Suddenly Chad perked up. "If we win, we can get that new floor!"

"Hey, that was the first thing I thought of." It was annoying to the whole team that the floor was in such bad shape. After all, they were champions! Their games were standing room only! They deserved floorboards that didn't buckle!

"So," Troy went on, "I just wanted to let you guys know what was up. Let's all go home and brainstorm. We can start our campaign first thing tomorrow. I'll call Gabriella tonight and make sure she and Taylor and the Decathlon team are onboard. Maybe we can all meet up at lunch and get this thing going."

"Right on," Zeke said, putting his hand out in front of the group, like they would in a team huddle. The others did the same, and soon there was a pile-on of hands.

"Let's do this!" Troy shouted, and they all broke away, cheering.